POCKET · PUFFINS

Puffin Books, Penguin Books Ltd, Harmondsworth, Middlesex, England
Viking Penguin Inc., 40 West 23rd Street, New York, New York 10010, U.S.A.
Penguin Books Australia Ltd, Ringwood, Victoria, Australia
Penguin Books Canada Ltd, 2801 John Street, Markham, Ontario, Canada L3R 1B4
Penguin Books (N.Z.) Ltd, 182-190 Wairau Road, Auckland 10, New Zealand

First published by Hamish Hamilton Ltd 1977
First published 1987 in Pocket Puffins
by Puffin Books in association with Moonlight Publishing Ltd
Copyright © Michael Foreman, 1977

Made and printed in Italy by La Editoriale Libraria

Panda's Puzzle
and his Voyage of Discovery

written and illustrated by
Michael Foreman

High in the mountains the winters are long, and in the summer very little sun gets through the thick bamboo forest to warm the earth.

In the forest lived a panda. A very young panda. He lived all alone as pandas do, and sometimes he wandered down the mountain to find delicious wild flowers and honey to eat.

One day Panda came upon a deserted camp site. Empty cans had been left behind by untidy travellers. Panda looked first at his reflection, and then at the pictures on the cans. The pictures were of ships and cities and scenes unlike any he had seen. There's more in the world than the ups and downs of mountain life, thought Panda.

One can, his favourite, had a picture of two large bears, one black and one white, standing amongst high buildings. "Am I a white bear with black bits or a black bear with white bits?" he wondered.

He turned his back on the cold, wet forest, and carrying the cans, he followed the tracks of travellers towards the warm low lands.

Presently he came to a big building full of music.

Inside were rows of musicians and singers.

Panda approached the oldest man on the highest pile of cushions.

"Is this the way to the city of tall buildings and bears?" he asked.

"This is the way to everything," replied the old man. "Join us. Do you want to play a drum or a horn?"

"I don't know" said Panda.

"Well, do you feel like a drummer or more like a horn player?" asked the old man.

"I don't even know if I feel like a white bear with black bits or a black bear with white bits," groaned Panda. "But if you don't know what you are, how can you decide on anything?"

"I don't know that either," sighed Panda, and with a sad wave to the musicians, he walked out into the sunlight.

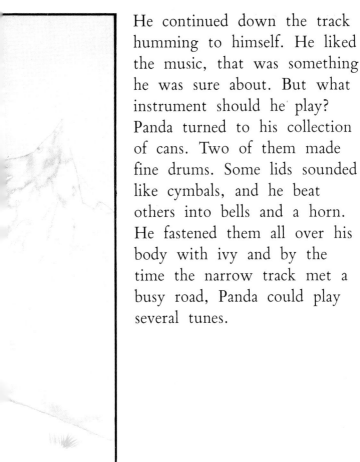

He continued down the track humming to himself. He liked the music, that was something he was sure about. But what instrument should he play? Panda turned to his collection of cans. Two of them made fine drums. Some lids sounded like cymbals, and he beat others into bells and a horn. He fastened them all over his body with ivy and by the time the narrow track met a busy road, Panda could play several tunes.

"Does this road lead to the city of tall buildings and bears?" he asked a wagon driver.

"It leads to a city, and you are welcome to travel with me. But I've seen no bears there," replied the driver.

"I've seen no bears anywhere," said the camel. "I just do my job. When I'm not working I get the hump. First I move my left feet, then I move my right feet, I'm good at it. Then I'm fed. I have a good life."

They moved slowly into the city.
Everywhere was bustle and noise.
Wonderful! thought Panda, there's more
to life than putting one foot in front of
the other.

Playing his tunes, Panda wandered
through the city until he came to a wide
rushing river.
"Does this river lead to the city of tall
buildings and bears?" Panda shouted to a
passing boat.

"It leads to the ocean," answered the boatman, "and the ocean leads everywhere!" Wonderful! thought Panda, and set about building a boat. He followed dolphins towards the setting sun, as flying fishes reflected the evening stars.

Panda smelt the flowers and sweet fruits
long before he saw land. Like all
seafarers, he reported his arrival to the
Customs Office.
At the top of the steps lay a lizard.
"This is my place," he told Panda,
"from here I can supervise all the
comings and goings. I can even look
down on that proud cockerel."

"I don't mind," crowed the cockerel,
"because from the church tower there is
always a cock looking down on the
lizard."

Would a black bear be higher than a
white bear? wondered Panda. And where
would *I* be? There must be more to life
than how high up you are, he thought,
and set sail once more.

For many months he sailed about the world, asking his questions in ancient timeless places.

"Best not to worry," said the leopard. "You cannot change your spots."

"Shsssssh!" hissed the snake, "I change my entire outfit."

"Some of us are just born superior," said the cow in a holier-than-thou voice.

"It's all a matter of background," said the chameleon.

"The important thing is to work to live," said the water buffalo. "Don't live to work. The best thing about working is stopping. I live for my evening wallow in the mud. The boy lives for his daydreams and grows a little heavier each day."
Panda just grew more and more confused.

At last Panda saw on the horizon the
tall buildings he had first seen on the
can.

"Now I will find the two big bears,"
cried Panda, and he rushed about the city

from the Customs Office, to City Hall, to the Information Office, but no-one could tell him whether he was black and white or white and black.

He went to the Central Library where they had books about everything. He was thrown out for making a noise.

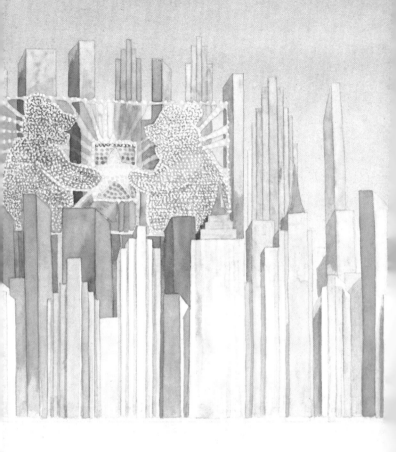

Sadly Panda sailed from the city. He
knew the big bears could tell him
nothing.
But perhaps everybody told him
something different because everybody *was*
different? Panda felt happier.

And when, once more, he was in the
building full of music, the old man
asked, "Have you discovered what you
are?"

"Yes," said Panda, "I'm a traveller who
plays tunes."

"So is the wind," said the old man.

"But are you a black bear or a white
bear?"

"I don't care!" laughed Panda. The old
man smiled.

"A great discovery!" he said.

And the music of that day joined the
music of the wind and blew from the
mountains to all the countries
of the world.

MICHAEL FOREMAN one day, while sailing in the West Indies, saw a lizard and a cockerel perched on some steps. At that moment, the idea for his picture book, *Panda's Puzzle*, sprang to mind.

Michael Foreman is a keen traveller and has visited China, the Himalayas and all the places to which Panda ventures (in fact Panda follows in Michael's own footsteps). Every picture in the book has stemmed from Michael's sketchbook of drawings and watercolours, all done "on location". You will even find the lizard and the cockerel as he actually saw them.

As well as beautiful paintings inspired by his journeys abroad, Michael Foreman has illustrated such prestigious authors as Dickens, Andersen, Grimm, Kipling... and Terry Jones, as well as the Bible. Many of his illustrations have also appeared in magazines. His work has won most of the sought-after awards for illustration, including the 1982 Kate Greenaway Medal, the Francis Williams Prize, for which he is now a judge, the Kurt Maschler Award and the Bologna Graphic Prize.

Michael Foreman, his wife and their two young sons share their time between London and Cornwall. However he continues to travel as much as possible.

*Self portrait by
Michael Foreman*

More Pocket Puffins for you to enjoy!

Bill and Stanley by Helen Oxenbury
A busy afternoon for Bill and his best friend,
Stanley the dog.

Peter and the Wolf by Sergei Prokofiev and Erna Voigt
The well-known musical tale, beautifully illustrated.

Mr Potter's Pigeon by P. Kinmonth and R. Cartwright
The touching story of an old man and his pet racing pigeon, with
award-winning pictures.

Billy Goat and His Well-Fed Friends by N. Hogrogian
Billy Goat doesn't want to end up as the Farmers supper…

This Little Pig-A-Wig by Lenore and Erik Blegvad
A lovely, lively collection of pig-poems old and new.

The Pearl by Helme Heine
Beaver realises that there are greater riches in life than even
the loveliest of pearls.

Fat Pig by Colin McNaughton
Fat Pig must lose weight. Somehow his friends just have to help
him…

The Feathered Ogre by Lee Lorenz
Little Jack the Piper outwits the ferocious ogre and plucks his
golden feathers. A very funny fairy tale.

If I Had… by Mercer Mayer
'If only I had a gorilla, a crocodile, a snake…then no-one would
pick on me…' A small boy's daydreams find a real-life solution.